Dedication

I would like to thank Jawad Yatim for introducing me to the sport of indoor football and encouraging me to write this book.

I am grateful to the Massachusetts Pirates' owners, staff and team, Lady Pirates, Pirates Nation and team members of indoor arena football teams for cheering me on during my medical ordeal.

Thank you, Isabella Jaeckel for illustrating this book!

Thank you, Erich Jaeckel for saving the day with your expertise in layout and design!

A shout-out to Judy Ruedinger, a true "cheesehead" and one of the kindest people I know. Judy always said I should make a living writing books and playing classical guitar. Better late than never, Judy!

A special thanks to my husband, James who encourages me to follow my dreams.

I am especially thankful to the doctors, nurses and staff at St. Vincent Hospital in Worcester, MA for not only saving my life but also for giving me back my quality of life.

A Star Named Wink

Wink is a tiny star with a lot of sparkle.

Wink shimmers yellow when happy and glad.

Wink twinkles blue
when lonely or sad.

Wink can turn white and shine brighter than a streetlight.

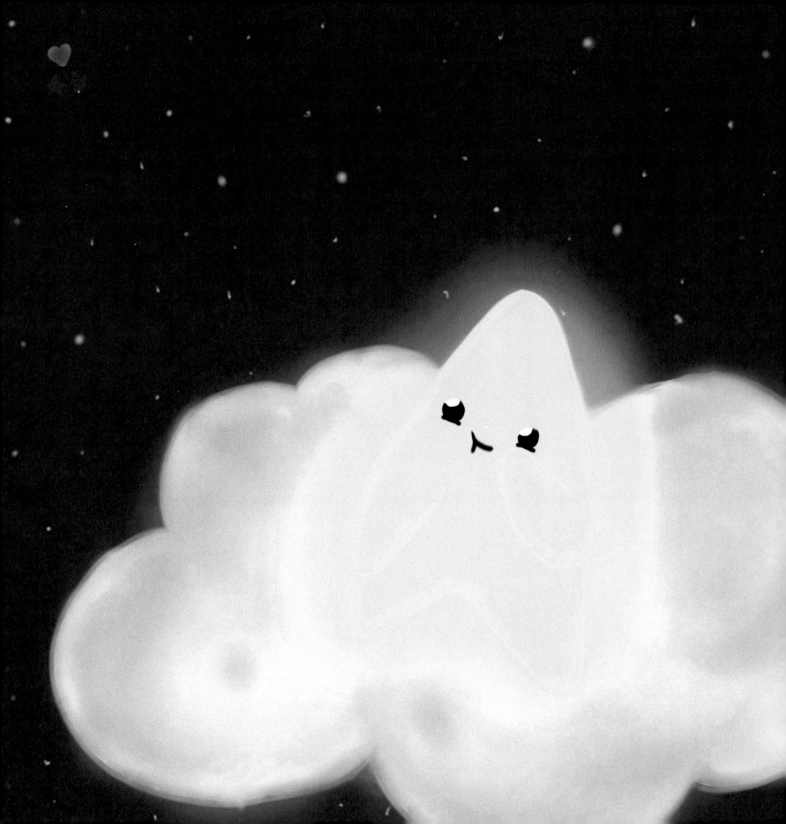

Wink turns many colors, but the star's greatest wish is to glow red when Wink finds a best friend.

Wink wonders, "How do I find a best friend?"

One evening, Wink hears a child ask, "Star, can you hear me?"

Wink shines streams of bright light down to earth.

The rays pass through the window of a brick house onto a boy with brown hair and brown eyes in red pajamas.

"Are you talking to me?"
Wink asks the boy.

"Yes," the boy giggles. "My name is James and my dog's name is Pirate because his black eye reminds me of a pirate's eye patch."

Wink tells James,
"My name is Wink."

James says, "I want to be on the flag football team. Tryouts are in three weeks. If I make a wish to be on the team will you grant my wish?"

Wink says, "James, I don't grant wishes, but if you work hard you have a chance of getting on the team!"

The next evening, Wink
watches James practice.

James runs in his back yard
with a football tucked under
his arm. Pirate barks and races
around the yard with James.

Wink sees James has red
cheeks. Wink gets an idea!

Every evening for three weeks, Wink swoops down to earth to play football with James and Pirate.

When James and Pirate are tired from running and practicing, Wink shows them loop de loops and twirls through the sky.

Something is wrong though. Wink still doesn't turn red but James gets stronger and faster.

The sparkly star wonders, "If James makes the team, will I ever see him again? Will I ever turn red?"

The night before the football team tryouts, Wink sees James is nervous. Wink tells James and Pirate to close their eyes for a second.

When they open their eyes they see sparkles of many colors fluttering across the sky like silent fireworks.

Wink says, "James, hold out your hands." James holds out his hands and a glittery speck gently floats down from the sky and lands into his cupped palms.

"Thank you Wink!" James says. The next day, James walks nervously to the football field with Pirate following behind him.

James quickly looks at the glowing gift from Wink and slides it back safely into his pocket.

The coach blows his whistle and tryouts begin!

That evening, James looks up at Wink and says with a big smile, "Wink! Thanks to you I made the team! Thank you for being my best friend!"

Then James says to Pirate, "Pirate! Look at Wink!"

Wink shines as red as a Valentine heart for the very first time, because the tiny star finally finds a best friend!

About the Illustrator

Isabella Jaeckel is 12 years old and lives in Massachusetts with her sister, parents, five chickens, one hamster and two fish. Her passion is art and she hopes to become a full-time illustrator when she gets older. Beginning as early as 6 years old, Isabella has been recognized and received multiple awards for her artwork. Her art was displayed at the Youth Art Month exhibit at the Boston Transportation Building, she was a winner of the nationwide Scholastic Picture a President drawing contest, and was a runner-up for Senator Gobi's Holiday Card Contest. When she's not drawing, you can find her hanging out with friends and family, acting in musicals, playing Roblox with her sister, and cuddling with her chickens.

42675986R00022

Made in the USA
Middletown, DE
19 April 2019